Mary & Joseph: A Christian Novel

Christian Youth Faith-Walkers Series

C.Orville McLeish

Published by HCP Book Publishing, 2024.

MARY & JOSEPH: A CHRISTIAN NOVEL

First edition. August 10, 2024.

ISBN: 979-8227690807

Written by C.Orville McLeish.

Also by C.Orville McLeish

Christian Youth Faith-Walkers Series
Detour: A Christian Novel
The Preacha And The Prostitute: A Christian Novel
Agents of Christ: The Prodigal Daughter: A Christian Novel
Chains: A Christian Novel
The Waiting Room: A Christian Novel
Chloe: A Christian Novel
Mary & Joseph: A Christian Novel

Made in God's Image Series
The Path to Spiritual Enlightenment
You Are Born To Win

The Unshakable Series
FAITH: A Theological Memoir

Standalone

Girl Unknown

Who I Am In Christ Daily Devotionals

How to Receive Your Healing

Sons of God: A Study on the Biblical Narrative of the Sons of God

Made in God's Image: We are Partakers of God's Divine Nature

A Glorious Church: In Pursuit of the Biblical Model of Christianity

The Seer: A Supernatural Christian Novel

The Soul of Man: Traversing the Mystery of Man as a Living Soul

Exit the Matrix: Embracing Our True Nature as Born-Again Christians

Watch for more at https://clevelandomcleish.com/.

Table of Contents

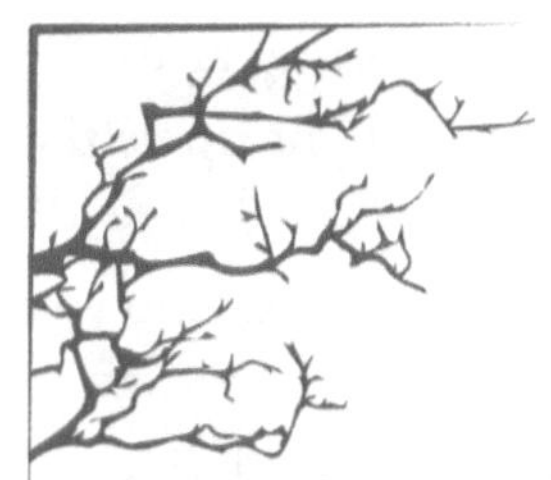

Chapter 1

"This child is destined to be the cause of the falling and rising of many in Israel. He will bring change to the world and He will be the cause of many hearts to be revealed. And a sword will pierce your own soul too."

As soon as the words were spoken, Mary felt hands grabbing at her arms and shoulders. Then she heard her mother's voice, but she couldn't make out the words. A part of her still wanted to hear the voice she'd heard earlier. The one that told her about the child who was going to change the world.

The hands that grabbed her now felt more urgent. "Mary! Mary! Wake up." The command definitely came from her mother. She slowly opened her eyes. Her mother towered over her. She felt her mother's urgent shake and then she again said, "Wake up, Mary!"

All her senses came alive and she sat up, completely alert, but being somewhere between reality and a distant memory of a voice that told her of things to come. She focused on her mother's face and slowly but surely lucidity set in. Mary jumped up and rubbed her forehead. It was only a dream, and it was over now.

"You were talking in your sleep again, Mary," her mother told her.

She leaned forward into her mother's comforting arms. "It was the same dream." The room had started to light up as the morning rays filtered through the small window.

Her mother held her close. "Maybe God is trying to send you a message," she said gently.

"It just feels weird, mother. Sometimes I can't tell what is real and what isn't."

"Just be patient, child. Whatever it is will reveal itself in due time."

She nodded and said obediently, "Yes, mother."

"Come on, let's get the day started," her mother said, and watched as Mary fussed around to tame her sleep ruffled hair. The troubled look was still in place, but just like the previous times, she knew Mary would recover soon. She was a special person. God really blessed her to have a daughter like Mary. *She warmed a mother's heart*, she thought.

Before she left Mary's chambers, she said, "I need you to go down to the cabinet maker later today. We need a new menorah stand. There may be some apprentices there, but make sure that you only speak to the person in charge."

"Okay, mom," Mary said.

"As soon as you've completed your chores, come to me. I'll describe exactly what I want. The carpenter would need to know the details."

IT WAS A LOVELY SUNNY day in Israel, and Joseph was doing what he loved most of all. He was recently trusted to run a carpentry workshop that belonged to his father. To him it was a true honor. The task was a responsibility that he didn't take lightly. His eyes darted to the other workers. He had to be a good example for them. Joseph looked at his tools. As a carpenter, he got to work with the most natural of things, and that was wood. Watching a tree stump morph into a block of wood, and then into a masterpiece was truly wonderful. To know that he was the inventor behind the masterpiece was a very rewarding feeling. Joseph stood back from the block of wood. It was as if he could see the finished product through it. All he needed to do was keep carving. The workshop was like a huge shed-like structure that allowed full view of the cobbled road.

"Hey, Joe, you know...me and the boys have been talking and...well, we don't want to come across as rude but, you know..."

Joseph looked up from his work and eyed Paul wearily. His friends knew better than to disturb him when he worked.

"What is it, Paul?"

"We were just wondering why we never hear you talk about a girl."

Joseph rolled his eyes. He knew exactly where the conversation was leading, and he didn't have the time or inclination to humor his friends. He wished that their fascination with his love life would cease. So what if everyone was already courting. Of course, those who were not courting were either married or not of age yet.

"I've had my sights on women," he said in a clipped tone.

"When?"

From his peripheral vision he saw James and Matthew approach, and he knew that they only came closer in order to join the discussion. It meant more jibes from them and even more defending from his side. The last thing he wanted was to be cornered, but here were his friends and fellow workers doing exactly that.

Joseph gave Paul a pointed look for starting with the dreaded topic.

"Look, Paul, I'm trying to work," he said and picked up the adz, which was his favorite tool in the workshop. The simple tool was used to roughly dress the wood. Its curved, chisel-like steel head was mounted at a right angle to the wooden handle and with Joseph's skills he was quickly able to transform a block of wood into a work of art.

When Joseph tried to turn his attention back to his work, he heard James' chuckle before he said, "That's all you ever do, Joseph. Take a break and have a conversation with us." The other two nodded as if James echoed their sentiment.

"I need to finish this," Joseph said, without looking up.

"That cabinet isn't due for another two weeks," this time it was Matthew who chimed in.

"We're all like brothers here, Joe," Paul said, "Yet you never talk to us."

Joseph looked up and said firmly, "Guys, I hate to waste a good day talking."

"Fine..," said Paul, "...then just answer the question and we'll leave you alone."

Joseph put the adz down and went to stand in front them. He was taller than them, and was towering over them as he said, "I am a God fearing man. I don't like to run around like you guys. I believe in that one special woman for me and I like to leave that space open for her."

"Hey," Matthew protested with mock innocence, "what are you talking about? We don't run around."

James jokingly elbowed Matthew and gave him a meaningful look as he laughed. "Yes, and we don't do anything more than looking. I don't want to be stoned," James added.

Joseph looked straight to him and replied, "I see many different women come here. I doubt if I have ever seen the same face twice."

"That's just where you're wrong..." responded James, "...Joe, you know that somebody has to take care of the ladies. As it is now, the odds are in our favor, five to one."

His response drew a frown from Joseph. He didn't care much for the conversation, but he was still curious about what James implied. "What odds?" he asked.

Matthew was the one who responded. "Oh, you know what he means. Caesar Augustus has been building up the cities and continued with many conquests. The men leave their homes, and some fall in battle."

His words were affirmed by a nod from James and Paul.

"So...," Paul added, "...for every one man there are five women...and I'm not talking about those independent types. I mean submissive, 'your every wish is my command' type."

James laughingly added, "It's a tough job, but somebody has to do it. I'll tell you this though, when you meet that one woman who turns your insides out, then you'll be hooked."

None of their statements were new to Joseph. Not only did he know all about what the Romans were up to, he'd also seen the effects on his people. The Roman hierarchy encouraged the Israelites to do the same. He knew that the Chief Priest was very important, but the Pharisees and Sadducees yielded a power of their own. Their influence on the laws that ruled them was known to all, but nobody challenged them. Just like nobody would dare to challenge Caesar Augustus. Joseph looked over at his workstation, wishing to get to the end of the discussion. "You all know me better than that. I am not interested in that kind of lifestyle," Joseph told them.

His answer excited Paul and he said as if he was about to pull a rabbit out of a hat, "It's why we're here!"

Joseph lifted his hand to stop whatever else Paul wanted to say. "Wait a minute. You all know what I believe, because I've said this before. There is a higher purpose for us being here. If you allow yourself to let thoughts of women creep into your head, then you'll struggle to fight temptation. It can also result in you missing that special one God has for you. You heard what the Rabbi said, didn't you? This is a taboo topic and you all know this."

His three friends had the decency to look away while nodding. They shifted uncomfortably.

Matthew was the first to speak, "Suppose she doesn't show up till you're sixty?"

"Well, I will still be right here, waiting," Joseph's reply was swift.

"You cannot be serious, Joseph..." said James, "...that's no way to live your life."

"It's my choice to make and I will be the one to live with the consequences."

"Okay, my friend," Paul said with a hint of mockery, "we appreciate the fact that you took a little time out to talk with us."

A chuckle came from Matthew when he said, "We're just glad to know that you haven't gone the other way."

They all exchanged meaningful looks.

"Which other way?" Joseph asked, sounding baffled and his question drew laughter.

"Our point exactly! You're not exposed enough to the real world, Joseph. You need to move out of your comfort zone," Paul told him, but Joseph ignored his words only to have James come up and pat him on the back and say, "You really think God is going to drop a special woman out of the sky right into your lap? Everyone knows that He helps those who help themselves."

Joseph chose to ignore that too, and this time he spoke with more force, "Hey! I really need to finish this if you guys don't mind!"

Once more they all looked at him, and then at each other, knowing that they were close to overdoing it.

James shrugged and walked away with the others falling into step beside him. Joseph watched them go. There were pros and cons about working in the workshop that was designed to cater for the community. *Having his friends to share his workspace was both a blessing and a curse*, he thought. James went back to the chest of drawers he was working on earlier. He picked up his bow-drill and got to work. Paul and Matthew moved in a different direction where they carved decorative pillars for an order that came in earlier that week. Even at their respective posts, their voices were loud enough to be heard by Joseph.

"He's hopeless," Paul was saying and James added, "Yeah. Case closed."

Matthew was the first one to notice the young women who were slowly making their way to the workshop. Paul noticed the mesmerized look on the face of his friend, and when he followed Matthew's gaze it was clear to see why his friend was captivated.

"My-my-my-my," Paul said softly, "...I think I'm in heaven, because I'm seeing angels coming my way."

At his words, James looked up and saw four young women who were chatting animatedly and giggling as they walked. He gave a low whistle as he watched them walk into the workshop area.

The young women stopped and looked at the men as if they knew exactly what was on their minds.

"May I speak to the one in charge please?" One of them said. The sound of her voice was in stark contrast to the harsh sounds of hammers, saws, bradawls and grinders.

Paul cleared his throat and stood up straight, "I'm in charge." He squared his shoulders and his chest went out a little.

She opened her mouth to address him, but before she could say anything Matthew said, "Don't listen to him, I'm in charge."

James jokingly chimed in, "They are both lying. I am in charge. What can I do for you?"

She looked at each one of them in turn. Her companions giggled.

Feeling shy and uncomfortable, Mary said with as much confidence as she could, "You can direct me to the one who really is in charge, please."

All three of them reluctantly pointed in Joseph's direction.

Mary looked over to the man who was still bent over his work. It was clear that he was oblivious to what was going on. She appreciated that about him. He clearly enjoyed what he was doing, and he was working with much gusto. The parchment her mother gave her with the order specifics was gripped tightly in her hand and she walked over to the man.

"Excuse me," she said, "are you in charge?"

For a minute she thought that he was going to ignore her, but then he put his tools down and dusted his clothes as he looked at her. When his eyes fell on her, his movements stopped and then he just stared.

Joseph looked at the young woman in front of him and felt an instant attraction. His emotionless face hid the turmoil that the sight of her created. *She was ravishingly beautiful,* he thought.

"Are you in charge?" she asked again, slightly louder as if she assumed that he didn't hear her the first time.

Joseph's mouth opened as if to speak, but closed again. A muscle jumped in his jaw.

On the other side of the workshop Paul frowned, and he studied Joseph. He noticed how Joseph carefully put his tools down without taking his eyes off the young woman.

Paul whispered loud enough for Matthew and James to hear, "If I didn't know better, I would think Joseph is awe struck."

James whispered back, "I think he is."

They were not speaking soft enough. Joseph tore his eyes away from her and looked at his friends. "Do you guys mind?" he asked, making them aware that they were not as quiet as they thought they were. However, the exchange helped to snap him out of his reverie.

All three of the men grinned guiltily, and Matthew spoke up, "This is a small workshop. We have no choice but to see and hear."

The three young ladies giggled again and whispered among themselves, being more successful in keeping their voices low enough not to be heard. One of them said something to the others and some more giggling followed.

Paul pointed to the young women and shrugged, saying, "See, everyone can see it. It's as plain as day."

Joseph rolled his eyes at him and then gestured for them to resume their work. They complied. Occasionally they looked up at the three remaining young women as they worked.

Turning back to the young woman in front of him, Joseph asked, "How can I help you?"

She explained, "We need a menorah stand with specific carvings on it. All the details are on here."

Then she handed him the parchment and Joseph took it. Their hands touched briefly and on reflex, Joseph snatched his hand back as if the contact had seared his skin. Their eyes met, but Mary looked away quickly.

Once again Joseph hid his emotions and scanned the parchment. On the one hand he wanted to know what the project entailed, but on the other hand he wondered whether she felt offended that he had snatched the parchment. He wondered if it made him look rude and coarse. He was neither, but for some reason he knew that her opinion mattered.

"The measurements are in there as well," she said, and he nodded. He liked the sound of her voice. His eyes quickly flicked up and for a moment he allowed himself to study her face. The moment was short-lived and he looked back at the parchment.

"I can make this stand."

"Good," she said, and then made an observation, "This must be hard work. Don't you get hot in all this heat, while you're working on all that wood?"

"It's hard enough," he replied wondering what she would think if he told her that it was not the heat of the day or the hardness of the work that affected him right then. He chose not to say a word.

She looked around the workshop as if she was looking for something else to comment on. Then she said, "My mother needs it done in two weeks. Can you do it by then?"

He smiled and dared to look at her again. "I can do it in five days," he said.

She gave him a bright smile and handed him the money while saying, "Okay. I will return in five days."

"Sure, that would be very nice," Joseph said, and as soon as the words were out, he wished that he had phrased it better.

She dipped her head down and smiled. It was a beautiful sight, and seeing her again in five days was a perk that he looked forward to."

"May I have a receipt please?" She asked and the question pulled him back from his thoughts.

"Yes...Yes! Yes, you can have whatever you want... Uhm..." Joseph bit down hard and a muscle jumped in his jaw. *He was putting his foot in it*, he thought, and tried to find something to say in order to make it right.

"Just the receipt, thanks," she said, and this time her smile turned into laughter. The sound was contagious and he laughed along with her at his silliness. Vaguely he registered that some of the other occupants in the room were commentating, but their words were lost to him. He quickly started to write a receipt on his parch-pad.

He paused and then looked up fleetingly to ask, "Can I have a name for the receipt please?"

"Mary...," she said, "...from the tribe of Judah."

"That's a nice name," Joseph said almost to himself and resumed writing.

He heard her giggle and say, "Yes, half the women in Jerusalem have it." Once again he felt that he'd said the wrong thing. He wondered what it was about her that had him tongue-tied and not able to rationally conduct himself according to his nature. Yet he couldn't help but to smile. She had that effect on him.

Still smiling, Joseph gave the receipt to Mary, but he made sure to touch the furthest corner of the parchment to avoid any accidental contact. He knew that she noticed his deliberate act when she looked at his hand for a moment longer than necessary before taking the receipt. His insides felt twisted. He was convinced that he'd insulted her.

"I'll see you in five days," she said and then left with her friends in tow.

Joseph looked at his hand. It was the hand that briefly touched hers earlier. Never before had one touch affected him so deeply. Something stirred within him again, just like it did when he first saw her. *That touch was one that he would never forget,* he thought.

It occurred to him that he may never want to wash this hand again.

"Wow," he said softly, having forgotten the other occupants of the workshop, but then he was quickly reminded of their presence when Paul said, "The mighty has fallen."

Confused, Joseph looked at him and asked, "What?"

"I've never heard you stutter before. Even when you talk about God or defend your faith, you never stutter. Then comes those chastening moments when we do wrong and yet no stutter.

But along comes a young woman asking you to make a menorah stand, and you stutter. Go figure."

"I did not stutter," Joseph said quickly in his own defense.

Paul threw his head back in laughter. "I have two witnesses that said you did. It can stand in court," he told Joseph through bouts of laughter.

Joseph shook his head. He had so much to make sense of, and defending himself to his friends didn't help him at all.

Matthew walked over to Joseph's work area and looked at the wood on the worktable before saying, "With all the work you have to do...," Matthew paused and looked Joseph in the eye as he asked, "how exactly do you plan to finish this in five days?"

"I can do it. I'll just work longer hours," Joseph told him.

"You already work sixteen hours a day, Joseph! Surely you're pushing it," said Paul.

Joseph picked up the adz and started to work again, mumbling, "So I will do twenty four hours."

Matthew shook his head. "Hmm, just to impress a girl?"

"Yeah, so tell us, what was that about?" Paul asked.

Joseph looked at the wood and tools in front of them, but for the first time his mind was not on what he had to do. She was from the tribe of Judah.

"She's the one," he told them.

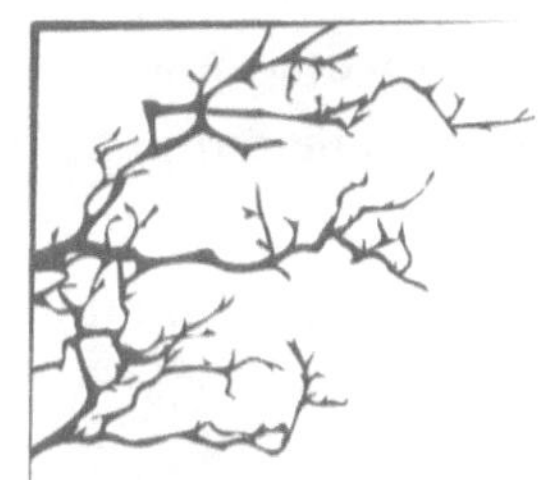

Chapter 2

Five days had passed, and Joseph felt exhausted. Matthew was right about his schedule, but the job he received from Mary was important to him. Every carve he made was with her in mind. It was easy to put the exhaustion aside and push forward. The menorah stand was finished and he had a mixture of anxiety and excitement at the thought of seeing Mary again.

He took a deep breath and continued to buff the menorah stand, even though he'd done so to perfection already. Needless to say, he considered it a miracle that he was able to finish all his work and also have time to add special touches to Mary's menorah stand. He really hoped that she liked it.

Joseph paused again. For some time now he had been rehearsing what he would say to Mary when she came to get the menorah stand.

Everyone was on a break, and he was alone in the workshop. Under normal circumstances, he would have savored the feeling, but his nerves didn't allow it.

He decided to practice out loud.

"Mary, I've been waiting all week...," he cut the sentence short, not knowing how to proceed. Then he tried again, "Here's your menorah stand. I can work on you next..." Exasperation made him grunt loudly. "Mary, can I see you again?" he asked into the empty workshop. He just didn't know at what point he would be able to ask her. Simultaneously he was acutely aware of the fact that she may not find him as appealing as he found her. *What if she rejected him,* he wondered.

He heard footsteps and spun around to see who was coming. It was Paul.

Joseph gave a heavy sigh. The morning had come and gone without Mary showing up. When the lunch hour arrived, he had hoped that she would come during that time and give him an opportunity to have some moderately private time with her. He knew that they would not be completely alone, but at least his friends wouldn't be there to goad him. She was, after all, a young maiden, meaning that she'd probably come with some of her friends again.

"You don't look like your normal self," Paul told him.

"I have a lot on my mind," Joseph answered.

"Of course you have. It's been five days since Mary was here...," he started, but Joseph lifted a hand to signal him to stop talking. He didn't want to be teased or made to defend himself again.

"Look, I've heard enough from you and the others. I'm having a hard time with this as it is."

"Sorry, Joseph. I guess I can't help myself at times," Paul said and then his face lit up as an idea came to mind, "Maybe you can give me and the guys the rest of the day off. This will make sure we stay out of the way when she comes."

Tempted by the idea, Joseph took a moment to think about it. Then his eyes went to their workstations, and he was reminded of the reason why the idea wouldn't work.

"We have deadlines. Remember the last talk we had? I told you that we needed to make sure we keep our word on everything. Customers depend on us to…"

"Yeah-yeah-yeah, I remember. It took you an hour to say what you could have said in less than ten minutes," Paul told him.

"Well, I had to make sure that it sunk in."

"Oh, it sunk in alright. I guess you're stuck with having us around the entire time then," Paul told him and then went to his workstation and started to rearrange the tools.

"Where's James and Matthew?" Joseph asked.

"They're at the market. They might be a little late, but they'll be here."

Joseph went back to buffing, and before long he was deep in thought. Once again wondering what he'd say to Mary when she arrived.

"She's coming," Paul said, and Joseph's head snapped up. His heart started racing painfully and he felt the lump form in his throat. His eyes went in the direction that Paul pointed.

There she was.

She looked every bit as beautiful as he remembered. He knew it was wrong to stare; at that moment it didn't matter.

It took a while for him to register the fact that an older woman accompanied her this time instead of her friends from the previous visit. It changed things. Of course it meant that she was raised well and it certainly confirmed her maiden status. Yet there was a part of him that wished the young women were with her instead. He would not get an opportunity to talk to her freely.

As soon as the women walked into the workshop, he went forward to greet them. Paul nodded his head politely to acknowledge their presence.

"You must be Joseph, son of Jacob," the older woman said, and then told him, "I'm Mary's mother."

Mary said a quick hello and then looked down.

"Yes, I am...," he responded, and said with his best business tone, "...it's a pleasure to make your acquaintance. Let me show you the stand. As soon as you confirm that you are happy with the way it looks, then I will start preparing it for delivery."

"That sounds good to me. I've looked forward to having this stand for a long time. A while ago I ordered a new menorah and I know I'll receive it before the next feast. It was so important to me that I had a stand to go with it...," Mary's mother said jovially.

Mary looked up and caught Joseph staring at her while her mother was talking.

She smiled.

He looked away and tried to focus on what her mother was saying.

"Were you able to get the inscriptions done?" Mary's mother was asking and Joseph forced his attention back to her.

"Yes, it's been added. Let me show it to you. Right this way," he said, and led the way.

Mary followed a few steps behind her mother. She'd been trying to keep her facial expression in check. Since meeting Joseph, she'd been unable to rid herself of the giddy feeling she got at the thought of him. She still remembered their brief touch. *It was clear that he felt the attraction as well,* she thought. Every single time their eyes met it felt like her insides were melting.

"Oh, this is simply lovely!" she heard her mother exclaim. Her eyes went to the menorah stand and then to Joseph. Once again he was looking at her, as if he was more concerned about her reaction than her mothers. She tried to hide the smile that pushed up from inside and threatened to overtake her expression. She lost the battle as the corners of her mouth lifted up.

"This is more beautiful than I could imagine, Joseph. You can arrange delivery," her mother said approvingly.

Out of necessity, he cleared his throat before he made any attempt to speak.

"What date will suit you for delivery?" he asked.

Mary watched as her mother became thoughtful, before saying, "Tomorrow afternoon. Mary's father will be home early and he'll help to position it just right."

He nodded, pleased at the idea of getting an opportunity to see Mary again. With the arrangements made, Mary and her mother left.

Seeing them go so soon didn't sit well with Joseph. The time that Mary and her mother spent at the workshop was all too brief, and he felt as if he was given something wonderful, only to have it snatched away before he could find any enjoyment from it.

"Seems like you're the one who will need to take the rest of the day off," Paul said.

Joseph didn't respond. The bright side was that he got to see Mary. There was one thing that he knew needed to be done, and that was to pray. He needed to hear from God and ask God to bless his decisions. *Surely God would not have created such deep feelings in mankind if it didn't mean anything,* he thought.

Regardless, he wanted to follow God. Joseph thought about one of the verses in the Psalms of David. *He leads me in paths of righteousness for His name sake.*

James and Matthew walked in. It was well past their designated time to return, but this was one time that Joseph didn't say anything. He ignored their guilty looks. Instead he stood at his worktable, trying to remember what his next project was. Every thought and energy had gone into the menorah stand for Mary. Now that the project was over, he had to reorganize himself.

"We heard that Caesar Augustus has decided to get detailed information from the people he governs," James sounded cautious as he spoke. It was as if he was testing the waters, and wasn't sure if Joseph was receptive to small talk.

Joseph wasn't interested, but felt that it was better than pining for Mary.

"Yeah?" was all Joseph said.

It was enough to encourage his three co-workers.

"That's right, there's talk about a count," James said.

Matthew shook his head and said skeptically, "I heard the same thing, but I don't see how he's going to get everyone counted. You shouldn't believe everything you hear, James. Unless Caesar Augustus sends out a decree, it's only gossip. There's no possible way that he could have everyone under his rule counted."

"Come on, there must be ways. He'll send someone to count the people," James defended.

This time Paul added, "Caesar owns too much land. It doesn't seem viable to do such a huge count."

"What would he want to do with all that information anyway?" Matthew asked.

Still defensive, James responded, "Paul said the other day that for every one man there are five women. Well, the count will prove that statement to be a fable or a fact."

"It's a fact," Paul insisted teasingly.

"We'll see," James told him.

"Like I said, unless Caesar Augustus sends out a decree, it's only gossip," said Matthew.

"You're right. I'm just curious about how it'll be done...," Paul started, "...I think it would be fun to see."

"It will be disruptive." The statement came from Joseph, and it had such finality in it that the others didn't respond immediately. Joseph added, "Matthew is right. Don't go after gossip. Counting people will just mean time away from work."

"That wouldn't be so bad," Paul said laughing, being unable to resist the comment.

"Yes, you're right about that. Besides, how bad can it be?" James responded, and for the first time he didn't sound as if he had to be the defender of the grapevine news.

"Alright everyone, get back to work. We still have a lot of work to get done," Joseph told them and then took his logbook. He still didn't know what his next project will be. It was important to stay busy so that he could control his thinking, and of course it would keep thoughts of Mary at bay.

JOSEPH AND PAUL ARRIVED at Mary's house at the designated time. As usual, they'd loaded the merchandise on the back of a donkey-pulled cart. Mary's father came out the minute he knew they were outside and helped to carry the menorah stand into the house. It was Mary's mother who had the final say on where the menorah stand would go.

Mary was nowhere to be seen.

"Let me get you fellows something refreshing to drink," Mary's father offered.

They accepted. For Joseph, it was the one opportunity he had to linger his stay in the hopes that Mary would arrive soon.

They spoke about general things. They spoke on topics that would normally have held his interest, but his distraction made it difficult to stay focused. Someone walked through the door, and his head swung around to see who it was. It wasn't Mary. He felt deprived, but one look at Paul made him realize that he missed something important. His gaze went to Mary's father, and he saw the look of expectancy. It was clear that a question was posed that he had yet to answer.

"Umm..., I'm sorry..., could you repeat that please...?"

Mary's father complied, "Chariot racing tomorrow. I asked if you would like to come along to the arena to watch it."

Caught off guard, he looked back to Paul and saw his friend give him the signal to say yes.

Joseph nodded quickly and said, "Of course that would... that would be nice."

"Good...," her dad responded and got up to signal the end of the visit, "...that settles it. We'll meet tomorrow at the races."

Joseph and Paul left soon afterwards.

MARY STOOD IN THE KITCHEN with her mother. It felt like torture to be so close, yet be unable to go out to see Joseph.

"They left," her mother told her and then went about preparing the evening meal.

Mary didn't say a word. Her thoughts were scrambled. Her mother continued, "His work is very good."

Still Mary didn't say a word. Instead she went through the motion of helping her mother prepare the meal.

"You like him, don't you?" her mother asked, and Mary looked up.

"Mom...," Mary started, but trailed off.

"I saw the way you looked at him at the workshop. Of course I saw the way he looked at you too."

"I don't know... I... yes... he's nice..." she stumbled over her words.

"It's okay. He looks like a good man, and you're of marriage age."

"Mom...!"

"I already spoke with your father about him. We'll see if your father approves."

Mary was speechless. For a moment she wondered whether her mother was just joking, but looking at her made it clear that she was completely serious.

"I just met him a few days ago," Mary said, not knowing whether to feel embarrassed or not.

"Sometimes one look is all it takes."

"Mom..."

"Mary, we're only making sure that nobody takes advantage of you. Any man would want to marry you, but that's not what we want. We want the right man to marry you."

"I'm not in a hurry to get married."

"Of course you're not. Nobody is saying you are. However, you need to consider the facts, my child."

"What facts?"

"You've blossomed into a beautiful young lady. There are different types of men out there."

Now she was discomfited, "I don't think we need to discuss this now, Mom."

"Why not?"

"Well...," Mary started, but had no idea what to say.

"And when will it be the right time? These things are important."

Mary conceded, deciding that it was better to just allow her mother to get it all out. Her mother didn't disappoint.

"Like I said, there are different types of men. Some of them are honorable, hardworking and will treat you like you are a precious jewel. But that's not all you want. It's important for that man to obey all the commandments of God. Someone who knows scripture..., someone who loves the God of Abraham, Isaac and Jacob... Someone like...," her mom thought about it for a while, and then added, "...someone like... your dad!"

"Like Dad?"

"Yes, your father has all those good characteristics. He reads the Torah every single day and follows the path that God has set out for His people."

"He's the best dad."

"Yes, he is. Now, I need to go on. There are also men who pretend. They go to the synagogue, and they act the way people expect them to, but their hearts are not right. These are the dangerous ones. They go against the Law of Moses. They seek worldly pleasure only. They will sweet-talk a beautiful young woman like you, but they won't look after you. But they act so well, that it's not possible to see the real person."

"I don't think that Joseph is like that."

"No, I don't think so either, but your father and I are here to protect you. We'll make sure that we look for any worrisome signs."

Mary went to her mother and threw her arms around her. "I love you, Mom. I know you and dad are doing your best for me. I also want the will of God to be what drives me."

"That's my girl. We'll wait to hear what your father has to say. Then we'll decide how to move forward."

BACK AT THE WORKSHOP Joseph was pacing back and forth. The sun had gone down a while back and he was all by himself. He'd been so sure that he would see Mary, and the disappointment didn't sit well with him. Never before had he felt that way about a woman.

It was here where his father, Jacob, found him.

"Everything okay, son?"

Joseph swung around and saw his father standing at the entrance.

"Yes – yes, of course. Good evening, Dad," he responded.

"We expected you home already. Your mother sent me to come find you."

The mention of his mother made him smile. *Yes, she was overly concerned for her family,* he thought. It didn't occur to him that anyone would be concerned when he didn't show up at home. Normally he was punctual and considerate, but that was before his mind was locked on Mary.

"I wasn't going to stay much longer," he told his father, not knowing how else he could explain his absence.

Jacob nodded to show his understanding, and looked ponderingly at his son for a while before he commented, "You don't look like you've been doing anything other than pacing all this time. What's bothering you?"

Instead of answering immediately, Joseph went to his workstation to collect his satchel. When he turned, his father was right there behind him, raising a brow as if to say, I'm waiting for an answer.

"It's nothing, Dad," he told his father.

In response, his father took the nearest chair and sat down with his arms folded, and giving a clear message that he wasn't going anywhere until the situation was sorted out.

Joseph knew that look well.

Then his father said the words Joseph had always heard from him when he wanted answers from someone. "Are we doing this the easy way, or the hard way?"

For years his father had used this method to encourage him to talk, Joseph thought. Of course he knew that the bottom line was to make it clear that whether it took a long or short time, talking was inevitable. He appreciated that about his father. For the most part, he found that it was more beneficial to get to the point as fast as he could.

Talking about a woman didn't come easy. Joseph stood looking at the floor.

Then his father spoke again, "It must be a big problem if it's eating at you this way."

Joseph pushed his hand over his face, saying, "It's nothing serious, Dad. I just have a lot on my mind."

Jacob stood up and placed his hands on Joseph's shoulders. Joseph avoided his eyes.

Then his father's face lit up as if the truth suddenly struck him. "I know that look," Jacob said with a smile that grew bigger and brighter as he spoke, "It's a woman."

Taken by surprise, Joseph met his father's gaze, wondering how his father could come to such a conclusion by just looking at him. Unable to hide it any longer, he nodded. "Yes," Joseph said the single word to confirm his father's suspicions.

The confirmation apparently resulted in making his father overjoyed, because the next thing he knew, his father patted him on the back and said, "Yes! This is cause for celebration."

"Don't you want to know about the woman first?"

"Of course, son! I want to know all about her. Your mother would too. We know you. We are confident that your choice would be from the top of the range. You make me so proud!"

"Thanks, Dad. I think"

"So? Now you can tell me who she is."

"Her name is Mary."

The name didn't ring a bell for his father, and then he asked, "What tribe is she from?"

"She's from the tribe of Judah."

"That's good-that's good! What about her parents."

"She's the daughter of Joachim and Anne."

"Yes! I know them!" his father exclaimed, and then he sat down as if all the excitement tired him out. "That's wonderful news. See, we told you that you would make a good decision."

Seeing his father's reaction helped Joseph to see things in perspective. What he felt for Mary was something to be celebrated, not something to be brooded on.

"So, we need to meet her parents. And then meet her too, of course," his father was saying as if he was thinking out loud.

"Her father invited me to go to the arena with him tomorrow. There's going to be a chariot race."

"Did you tell him how you felt about his daughter?"

"No."

"Then good for him! It is a wise move to invite the man over who brings a twinkle in his daughter's eyes. It clearly means that he knows how Mary feels about it. It's a good sign."

His father's words sunk in. Then it suddenly occurred to him that this knowledge could have been the reason why he didn't see Mary. Joseph smiled. Her father was sizing him up, and saw it fit to invite him for a second meeting.

"We need to get home or your mother would come out here herself to look for both of us."

"Yes, of course, Dad."

"Then we need to let her know. She's going to be thrilled. I'm sure she'll want to reach out to Mary's mother soon."

"Surely it's too soon."

"Why? Do you think you're going to stop loving Mary tomorrow?"

"No, that's not what I meant."

"What about her? From what I understand, her parents have gotten the ball rolling. So the question is whether you think she has feelings for you."

"I think she does."

"Then there's no reason to hesitate. Boldly step out and do what you believe is right. Always be honorable. This is an important step in your life," his father said and then patted Joseph on the back again before adding, "Let's go home."

The walk home was short, and feeling a lot more at ease, Joseph spoke about the upcoming projects at the workshop.

This was how they entered the house. They were deep in discussion about woodwork and the best carpentry methods.

"There you are!" his mother exclaimed the minute they walked in and then went on to tell Joseph's father, "This message came for you."

She handed him a parchment, which he quickly opened and read.

Grinning from ear to ear, he looked to Joseph and said, "Seems like I'm clearing my day tomorrow. I've been invited to go to the chariot races with you."

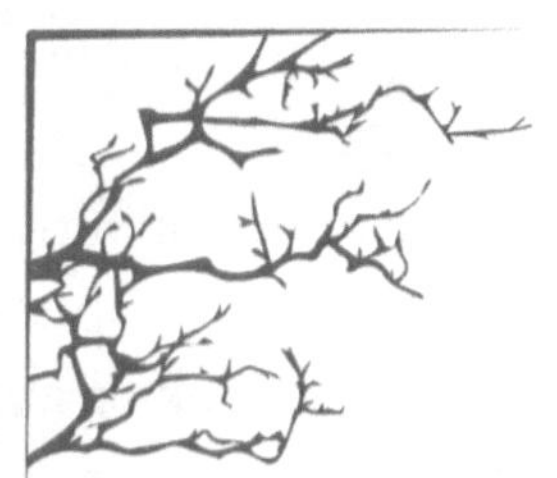

Chapter 3

Mary woke up feeling more excited than ever. She was told about the chariot race. The men would go to the arena while the women prepared a meal for their return. It meant that she was guaranteed to see Joseph. This was confirmed by her mother who told her to take extra care with her appearance.

The morning dragged along slowly. Soon it was time for her father to leave, and she wished that he would agree to take her along.

"There are many wise words in our scriptures. Think about the Proverbs that deals with patience," her father told her.

The words were spoken kindly, but it didn't take away her eagerness to go. Mary didn't argue the point, and obediently waved as he left.

Meanwhile her mother had started work in the kitchen and before long Mary's time was swallowed up with all the cooking.

Finally, the hour arrived that marked the return of the men.

Mary was a bundle of nerves.

Their arrival was rowdy. The two older men were chatting up a storm and exchanging their accounts of what transpired at the arena. On the other hand, Joseph's contribution to the conversation was a lot more subdued. He laughed along with them at jokes, and would nod wherever needed, but for the most part he'd allow the older men to run the exchange. His thoughts were elsewhere.

They were guided to the dining table. Mary came out with serving dishes laden with food and placed them on the table. Nervously, she placed them on the table and dared to look up at Joseph. It was clear that he had stopped any pretense of interest he had in the older men's conversation. Instead, he was looking at Mary, unable to help himself.

Her head dipped low and she smiled shyly.

Mary's mother came out of the kitchen carrying more serving dishes, and placed them on the table.

"Mary," her mother said gently, "There's one more serving dish in the kitchen. Bring it to the table, so we can open the table in thanksgiving to God."

"Yes, Mom," she said, and hurried off to the kitchen. But it wasn't long before she managed to steal one more look at Joseph.

Before long, they were all sitting down to enjoy the meal, and Mary's father was playing the role of a brilliant host. As the adults orchestrated, Mary was sitting next to Joseph, and it was the first time they were able to talk since their first meeting.

Their conversation started out awkwardly, as both of them didn't know what to say, but soon Joseph got the ball rolling. He asked her about her interests and gave her information about his in turn. Soon they'd covered many other topics.

At some point Mary's father had to remind them to eat, and they did their best to comply, but both of them didn't appear to have much of an appetite.

The older folks feigned oblivion.

THE RACES WERE THE first of several planned outings. Every time Joseph and Mary got an opportunity to spend time together, on every occasion they were accompanied by one or more people, predetermined by their parents.

They spoke about everything under the sun and discovered the many things they had in common.

There were long discussions about God and the importance of His laws. Part of their talks was to share their best scripture from the Torah. These were the talks that the two of them enjoyed most.

In all the time together, Mary never told him about her dreams. It just never occurred to her that it may be something he would be interested in. On top of that, she still couldn't make sense of it all, no matter how hard she tried.

Eventually the inevitable happened.

By mutual consent, and to the pleasure of their parents, they were betrothed.

In the weeks following their betrothal, their encounters were still carefully orchestrated, but neither of them minded. They understood the protocol and various laws that needed to be followed.

After a day at the open air Roman theatre where they watched jesters' theatrical entertainment, and many more events, Mary flopped on her bed in exhaustion. The day had been long, exciting and very memorable. She smiled. The thought of their impending marriage always made her spirits soar.

The last noises in the house subsided, signaling that everyone had gone to bed. For a while she stared at the ceiling, trying to imagine what her wedding day would be like. It was one of the most special days for a young woman. She thought about the feast, the guests and what foods she'd want to have prepared for the day.

All of a sudden, a bright light shone in the room. It shone brighter than the sun and left no shadow anywhere. Startled, Mary sat up on the bed. She didn't remember falling asleep, and she knew that it could not be a fire either. Frightened, she quickly made her way to the door, but the handle wouldn't budge. Fear escalated a few more notches.

"Rejoice, highly favored one, the Lord is with you. Blessed are you among women!"

Mary felt like she was about to jump right out of her skin when she heard the voice, and with lightning speed she spun around to face whoever it was.

A large man stood there. His clothes were white, and in the brightness of the room it looked like it shimmered.

"W... who..." paralyzed with fear, she was barely able to speak.

"I'm an angel, sent by God," he told her.

Her mouth opened and closed without a sound coming out.

The angel continued, "My name is Gabriel. God sent me to you."

"M...me...?"

"Yes. You're betrothed to a man whose name is Joseph."

"I... am..."

"You are of the house of David, now living in Galilee. The city named Nazareth."

"That's right," she said softly, still feeling thunderstruck.

"Don't be afraid, Mary...," the angel Gabriel started saying, "...for you have found favor with God."

"Favor with God..." she repeated.

"Yes Mary. I've been told to let you know that you will conceive in your womb and bring a Son into the world. You are to call His name Jesus."

"Jesus...," she said, again repeating what she heard.

The angel Gabriel nodded, and then continued, "Jesus will be great. He will be called the Son of the Highest. The Lord God will give Him the throne of His father David."

Mary's hand went up to cover her mouth and stifled the gasp before it could escape. All the while she listened and wondered if all this was some sort of dream. *Or perhaps a mistake,* she wondered.

The angel said, "He will reign over the house of Jacob forever. Of His kingdom there will be no end."

"But..., but...," she was still trying to make sense of it all. *If all this wasn't some mistake, then she would be the mother of the Messiah,* she thought. More and more things raced through her mind, including the fact that her life was going to be much different from what she had imagined. *What about Joseph,* she wondered.

"Jesus. His name will be called Jesus...," Mary whispered.

God didn't make mistakes, her heart told her. If the angel said that God had chosen her, then that was exactly what it is going to be. She looked at the angel as if to make sure that she wasn't dreaming, and then she asked the one question that was prominent in her mind.

"How is all this possible? I haven't been with a man."

The angel answered, "The Holy Spirit will come on you. The power of the Highest will overshadow you, Mary. It will be this way in order for the Holy One who is to be born, to be called the Son of God."

She heard the angel's words, and did her best to force some calm into her thoughts.

The angel spoke again, and said, "Now, Elizabeth your relative has also conceived a son, even though she is old. She was barren, but now at the age of sixty, she's with child. As you can see, there is nothing impossible for God."

His last words ricocheted through her head. She knew it was true.

She lifted her head and said with all the confidence she could muster, "Behold the maidservant of the Lord! Let it be to me according to your word."

As soon as she said the words, the angel disappeared and the light started to fade until the room was cast once more in darkness.

Sleep was elusive after that. She only made one attempt at it, but then gave up trying. She knew it was real. Deep down she knew without a shadow of doubt that God was going to work everything out. She didn't understand everything, but she trusted Him.

Mary thought about everything that the angel Gabriel said.

By morning, she knew what she needed to do, and she was eager to get to it. Even though she knew that the path would not be an easy one, Mary was determined to do the will of God.

For now, she wanted to visit Elizabeth. She remembered the angel spoke of her pregnancy. In itself, that was a miracle.

Elizabeth was much older than Mary. *She was old enough to be considered well over the child bearing age,* Mary thought.

The desire to visit her relative presented some more obstacles. The distance between Nazareth and the hill country of Judah was at least a week's journey. There was no possibility of leaving the house for weeks without telling her parents what was going on.

By noon, her parents knew the truth.

The conversation was hard on her, but knowing her nature, and believing in the sovereignty of God, they were standing with her in support.

"You won't be able to make the journey on your own," her father told her, "Your mother and a bondservant will go with you."

"What about Joseph?" her mother asked.

It was Mary's father who answered, "He has to submit to the will of God."

So it was agreed, and by that afternoon they set off on their journey.

Thoughts of Joseph weren't far from her mind. She had no idea how he would react, but she also knew that her father was correct. *Even so,* she thought, *time would tell how things would unfold.*

Part of her was excited about seeing her relatives.

When they arrived in Judah, they were met by Zacharias.

"It's wonderful to see you," Mary's mother said in greeting.

"Is Elizabeth here?" the question came from Mary.

To utter amazement, they discovered that he couldn't speak.

Zacharias gestured for them to go into the house.

Inside the house, Elizabeth heard Mary's voice, and felt movement in her womb as the baby leaped.

Elizabeth was immediately filled with the Holy Spirit, and then she spoke loudly. "Blessed are you among women, and blessed is the fruit of your womb. But why is this granted to me, that the mother of my Lord should come to me?" Elizabeth said and rubbed her stomach as she continued, "For indeed, as soon as the voice of your greeting sounded in my ears, the baby leaped in my womb for joy. Blessed is she who believed, for there will be a fulfillment of those things which were told her from the Lord."

She opened her arms and Mary walked into the embrace.

"Come, sit down...," Mary's mother said, "...we have a lot to talk about."

"You're right. These are great times. Praise be to God for His mercies," Elizabeth said.

Zacharias sat down with him and scribbled a note for them to read.

Thank you for being here. Elizabeth has three months left before the child is born. It would be an honor to us if you would stay with us for a while.

"Yes, of course I'll stay here," Mary said eagerly.

Her mother nodded her consent and said, "Go ahead, Mary, I'll return home in a few days, and explain to your father."

Overwhelmed by the greatness of God, Elizabeth said, "What a miracle! Because of God's mercy, I can have a child even though I'm this old."

Zacharias smiled and nodded. His face showed the awe and reverence he felt towards God.

"We exalt His name for all He does!" Mary's mother said.

Mary looked at them, and said, "My soul magnifies the Lord, and my spirit has rejoiced in God my Savior. He has regarded the lowly state of His maidservant. From this day forward, all the generations will call me blessed. The Lord God Almighty has done great things for me. Holy is His name! His mercy is on those who fear Him from generation to generation. He has shown strength with His arm. He has scattered the proud in the imagination of their hearts. He has put down the mighty from their thrones, and He exalted the lowly. He has filled the hungry with good things, and the rich He has sent away empty. He has helped His servant Israel, in remembrance of His mercy, just as He spoke to our fathers, to Abraham and to his seed forever."

When she had finished, she saw the tears of joy running down her mother's cheeks as well as that of Elizabeth.

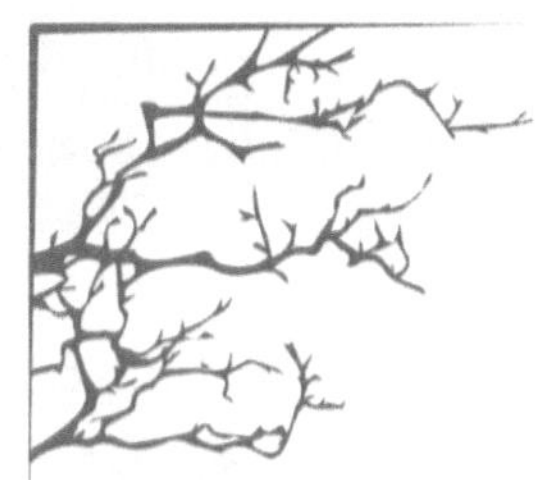

Chapter 4

"What do you mean she's gone?"

Joseph looked at his father and wished with all his heart that he could give a good answer to that question.

They had just completed their dinner, and he thought it was the best time to make the revelation.

"Paul told me that he saw her leave," Joseph replied.

"That doesn't mean anything. She could have seen someone off. Surely she would have told you that she was leaving," his father answered, and then shifted to make himself comfortable. Then he rubbed his belly as if to say that the barrel was full.

"I thought the same thing. So I went to their house, and was met by her father," Joseph told him,

"And?"

"She's gone."

Frowning heavily, Joseph's father asked, "What exactly did her father say?"

"Mary went to the hill country of Judah. Her mother and a bondservant went with her."

"Why didn't she let you know about it? One of these days you'll be married, and neither one of you can just leave whenever you want to. I would never have allowed your mother to leave so close to our wedding day..." Joseph's father trailed off. The frown was still in place.

"I don't know what to say, Dad. Of course I'm disappointed, but there's also a part of me that feels that she wouldn't have gone if it wasn't important."

"Yeah, but it still doesn't look right."

"I know."

"Perhaps I should go to Joachim and talk to him about it."

"It's okay, Dad. I don't think that it's going to make any difference now. It will be a week to get there, a week to get back, and then some days for the visit. I think she'll be back in less than a month."

"Joachim should never have allowed her to go. There are preparations for the wedding that still need to take place," Joseph's father said and then smiled broadly at the thought of the impending event and added, "Your wedding ceremony will be one of the best ones."

The smile was contagious. Joseph felt the tension ease up.

He still thought about Mary, but he preferred to think that she had a good reason for leaving without telling him.

Everything was going to be alright, he thought.

Joseph spent the rest of the evening talking to his father about the workshop. They discussed current projects, as well as upcoming ones. At some point the conversation changed and they spoke about the Torah. It was a favorite topic in the house. As always, they started to compare their current circumstances with that of the ancient times. They discussed some of the characters in the Torah, talking about things they could learn from the reaction of those in the ancient times.

Yes, Joseph thought, *everything will work out well.*

The following days all fused together. Mary was never far from his mind, and he couldn't wait to see her again.

Three weeks came and went, and Joseph started to expect news of her return.

For the first time he fully understood what his colleagues meant about being hooked. Every time someone walked into the workshop, his head would snap up expectantly. Every single time he had been disappointed.

An even bigger disappointment came when he discovered that Mary's mother had returned alone. Joseph felt tempted to go to their house and demand some answers, but he knew that it would go against protocol.

Mary's journey to the hill country of Judah was against protocol, he thought, but immediately rebuked himself. *Mary was the woman that he was going to marry,* he thought, and the last thing he wanted to do was to have bad thoughts about her.

Once the initial disappointment subsided, Joseph attacked his work with extra vigor. In his heart, he was talking to God.

He was acutely aware of the glances from his colleagues. He knew that Paul would have told them about Mary's journey, and he appreciated the fact that none of them breached the subject in front of him. Instead, he saw them all bent over their work as if they were driven in the same way he was. *It was their way of letting him know they understood what he was going through,* he thought.

Two months after Mary left, Joachim invited Joseph's father over for a meal. On his father's return, Joseph tried to get as much information from him as he could.

"When is Mary coming back?" he asked.

His father shook his head and answered, "We didn't talk about Mary, so I don't know when she'll be back."

"What do you mean? Why did they invite you?"

Joseph's father shrugged, and looked at his son with empathy as he said, "It was just normal procedure for the father of the bride and the father of the groom to spend time together."

"That was it?"

"Yes, son, that was it. I couldn't ask what they didn't volunteer. They appeared to be in good spirits."

"It's been two months..."

"Patience, son. That is what you need to have right now."

"It's not easy."

"Of course not," Joseph's father told him and he went on to say, "That is why we need God. Remember what the Torah said about patience. If Sarah waited patiently for God, then she would not have given Abraham another woman to have Abraham's child. Patience plays a big role when it comes to faith."

Joseph nodded, grateful for the pillar of strength that his father always proved to be. Yet, nothing could prepare him for the time when Mary finally arrived.

MARY HAD STAYED IN the hill country of Judah for three months, and on her return home, Joachim called for him.

The minute Joseph received the message, he dropped everything he was doing.

His eagerness and excitement to see her was immediately stumped when he saw her.

Yes, Mary was back, but there was something different about her. There was an earnest look in her eye that came close to pleading, but he didn't understand why she would look at him like that.

Of course he forgave her for not telling him about the trip, he thought, and he was about to reassure her that everything is fine. Before he could say a word, Mary's father spoke.

"Joseph, when I met you, I knew immediately that you were an honorable man. You are a man who follows the statutes of Yahweh. There's something that you need to know," her father said.

Mary's mother was seated next to Mary, as if to give her support, but even in that, Joseph didn't understand the need.

It was when Mary stood up and walked to him that he noticed the changes in her body. He searched her eyes, but his stomach clenched up. *None of it felt good,* he thought. It was all wrong. She was supposed to look ecstatic to see him. At the very least, she should have mirrored his joy.

"There's something you need to know, Joseph," she started, "It's the best news that I could have ever received."

"Then why do you look as if there's bad news that you want to share?" Joseph asked.

"The news is good, but I don't know what it will mean for our future. I fear that it will not make you as happy as it should."

"What is it, Mary?" he asked, hoping that she would come to the point quickly. The anxiety was growing at a phenomenal speed.

"An angel of God came to me and told me that the Messiah was going to be born," Mary told him and watched as his eyes lit up.

"The Messiah? The Promised One?" Joseph remembered all the scriptures that referred to the coming Messiah, and his countenance cleared.

"Yes," Mary said and nodded.

"That's great news! When is He coming? Where is He now?" Joseph asked, believing that a great warrior had been chosen by God to redeem His people and finally save them from the Roman rule.

"He's inside me," came the soft answer from Mary.

"What?!" Joseph wasn't sure if he heard correctly. He frowned and leaned closer to make sure he heard and understood correctly when she repeated herself.

"The angel said that I would give birth to the Messiah. I'm pregnant."

He looked at her for a moment as if she'd grown horns. So many thoughts went through his head, and none of them was something he could make sense of.

"Pregnant..." he started and staggered back as if he wanted to get away but couldn't find the strength to do so.

"Yes, I'm having a baby."

"I thought you were a virgin?"

Her eyes went down and she looked embarrassed, "I am."

"You can't be. Virgins don't become pregnant, Mary."

"I..., God...," she faltered.

His eyes went to Mary's parents and it was clear that this was not a prank. There was no humor in their gaze. For a moment anger clouded his better judgment as he spoke.

"Were you pregnant before you left for Judah? Is that the reason you left without any explanation?"

"Joseph, I told you...," she started, but he interrupted.

"Or did you get pregnant there in Judah? And please tell me why you would use God as an excuse?"

"Joseph!" like a whiplash Joachim called out his name. Joachim continued, "I've never had a reason to doubt my daughter's word. She loves the Lord just as much as you do. Look at her Joseph. It's an honor for her to be chosen."

Joseph hung his head, not knowing what to feel.

"Where does that leave me?" Joseph asked.

"You're betrothed," Joachim told him.

"And she's pregnant," Joseph said. All anger had left him, but in its place was a bitter and gut-wrenching feeling instead.

"I carry the child gladly. I know what it looks like, but I also know that it is God Himself that has done this. I've never..., never...," she trailed off, being unable to even say the words.

"Whether you're right, or wrong, it still doesn't answer the question I asked. Where does all this leave me?" Joseph repeated.

"If you leave her now...," this time it was Joachim who couldn't finish the sentence. He knew what it would do to Mary. He also knew what it would do to his family.

"I have to go. I need to think," Joseph said, and before any of them could say anything, he was gone.

Joseph ran. He didn't know what direction he took and he didn't care either. At some point, he felt the burning in his chest, but just kept going. Even with all the running, his thoughts stayed with him.

He thought about what he should do. He thought about her trip to the hill country of Judah. He finally understood the look she gave him when he walked into their house. She looked vulnerable. He knew that now. In addition, he knew the reason for that look.

One of the most overwhelming feelings he had was a sense of betrayal. She was either the biggest con artists he knew or what she said was true.

Joseph came to a panting halt. He vaguely registered the fact that he was several miles away from home. Standing there, out of breath, the thought came up again, and he wondered what if she was telling the truth.

If she was carrying the Messiah, then how could he publically humiliate her? Besides, he didn't like public scenes, and he didn't want to be in the middle of a scandal.

The only thing that made sense to him was to quietly break off the engagement. *If her father was clever,* he thought, *then he would send Mary away so she could have a life without ridicule somewhere else.*

No matter how he felt, or what injustice he believed was done against him, he was still an honorable man, he thought. He would give as much protection to her reputation as he could. He would put her away secretly.

Feeling a little better, Joseph believed that he had just came to the most reasonable conclusion.

With this resolution in mind, Joseph made his way home.

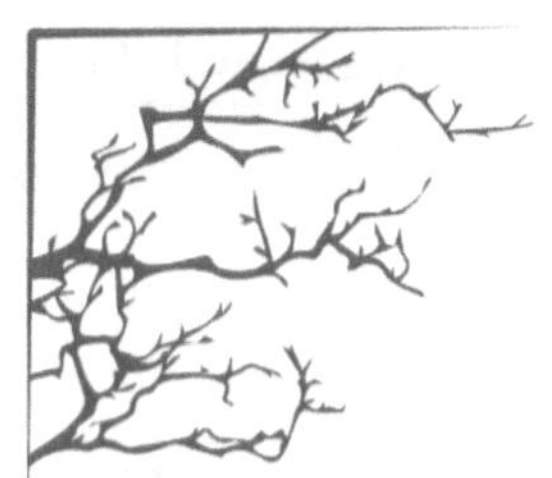

Chapter 5

B y the time Joseph made it home, he found the house in darkness. It was late at night, and his parents knew that he went to see Mary. It was obvious they thought that everything was going well, and didn't see the need to wait up for him.

He went straight to his room, feeling drained. It wasn't only the running, but also the emotional turmoil that took a toll on him.

Lying on the bed, fully clothed, he fell asleep.

"Joseph, son of David, do not be afraid to take to you Mary your wife." Joseph heard the voice and then saw an angel standing in front of him. Amazed, he listened as the angel spoke, "That which is conceived in her is of the Holy Spirit."

"So, she told me the truth?" Joseph asked and the angel nodded.

"Mary will bring forth a Son, and you shall call His name Jesus. He will save His people from their sins," the angel said.

It was as if scales fell from the eyes of Joseph as he listened. He remembered the scriptures referring to a virgin giving birth to a boy. It was from the book of Isaiah.

Looking at the angel, he quoted the verse, "Therefore the Lord Himself will give you a sign: Behold, the virgin shall conceive and bear a Son, and shall call His name Immanuel. That is from Isaiah seven verse fourteen."

"Yes," the angel said, "the name Immanuel is translated, 'God with us'" and with those words, the angel disappeared.

Joseph woke up.

The sun was streaming through the opening in the wall and smells from the breakfast table reached him.

He wasn't hungry, and all fatigue had left him. In no time he was back at Mary's front door.

Joachim rushed to open the door after he heard the urgent knocking.

Joseph stood in front of him with a foolish grin on his face.

"May I please have your daughter to marry and love for always?" Joseph asked.

Joachim's face lit up and he drew Joseph inside to the kitchen where Mary and her mother stood working.

The minute she saw him, she knew. Joseph opened his arms, and she ran into his embrace.

"An angel appeared to me in a dream. I'm going to stand with you, It's a huge responsibility to raise a child, and you don't have to do it alone."

Joachim stood next to his wife and wrapped an arm around her shoulders, as he looked at the two young people. He saw it as a great honor to have his daughter chosen to carry such a precious cargo. He was grateful towards God for allowing Joseph to be the man to take care of Mary. *He had proven himself to be an honorable man indeed,* Joachim thought.

Together with Mary and her parents, Joseph went home and had a discussion with his parents. True to his nature, his father didn't say a word until he felt that he had heard every aspect of the matter. When Joseph finished his explanation, the house fell silent.

Joseph's father stood up quietly and went to stand next to the menorah stand. He opened the showcase-cabinet and took out the Tanakh scroll.

Then he carried the scroll over to the table and opened it on the scriptures from Isaiah the ninth chapter. Using his finger he brushed over the words and came to a stop at verse six.

Then he read out loud, "For unto us a Child is born. Unto us a Son is given. And the government will be upon His shoulder. And His name will be called Wonderful, Counselor, Mighty God, Everlasting Father, Prince of Peace."

Joseph's father closed the Tanakh scroll. Nobody moved. Nobody said a word as he put it back in its place. Then he turned to Mary and looked at her for a while.

"You have been chosen. We will do everything we can to help and support you," Joseph's father said.

It was like a cloud had lifted.

"We can arrange the marriage," Joseph said, "but I believe we need to do it quietly."

"Of course. And the sooner we do it, the better it will be." Joachim agreed.

It was agreed.

Joseph and Mary got married. Out of reverence to God, they didn't consummate the marriage. Keeping Mary comfortable, and at ease was Joseph's main priority.

There was a change coming to the nation of Israel, he thought. Just the knowledge of having such a wonderful miracle to take place in his lifetime was remarkable. Yet this was even better. It wasn't only in his lifetime, but it was also taking place in his household. It was something that he thanked God for.

Something else was happening that would change the course of events.

One day, as the family was sitting down to dinner, Joseph's father broke the news to them.

"There's been a decree from Caesar Augustus. He wants the people to be counted."

As had been the case for some of the nights since Joseph reaffirmed his commitment to Mary, both families had their dinner together. The implication of what Joseph's father was saying settled in.

"I heard some rumors to that effect a while back, but I thought it was just a figment of someone's wild imagination," Joachim responded.

"How does he plan to do that?" Mary's mother asked.

"Well, everyone needs to register in their own city,"

"We're of the house of David, that means we're to go to Bethlehem," Joseph responded thoughtfully. His eyes went to Mary who was toying tenderly with her stomach. She appeared oblivious to the conversation, and more importantly, the implication.

"Surely there'd be other ways to do it that wouldn't involve uprooting people and having others displaced this way," Mary's mother commented.

"It's Caesar we're talking about. What Augustus Caesar wants, is exactly what Augustus Caesar will get," was the response from Joseph's father.

"When does he want all this to happen?" Joseph asked.

"Most people will be making plans as soon as tomorrow," his father replied.

"What about the business. This is going to cost us a lot of business," Joseph protested.

His father shrugged, and then told him, "Nobody has a choice in the matter."

The room became quiet while each one was wrapped in their own thoughts. As for Joseph, his thoughts mulled around freely, but then divided between Mary's delicate condition and the woodwork projects that he had to complete.

"I don't mind the journey at all. Bethlehem is only about a four-day journey away from here," Joseph's mother said and everyone nodded, except Joseph.

"It'll probably be double that time in order to make sure Mary has as little discomfort as possible," Joseph said, and again everyone nodded and looked at Mary. She smiled back, wondering what it was that she had missed.

Joseph returned her smile to reassure her, and then said to his father, "It would be possible to finish off a few more projects before leaving. The delay wouldn't make much of a difference."

"I wouldn't be too sure of that, son," his mother told him, and then explained, "the tribe has grown substantially. A lot of people will be flooding Bethlehem. You would want Mary to be well taken care of while she's there."

His mother was right, he thought and just nodded. There was still a part of him that believed the short delay would be acceptable.

Joseph discovered just how wrong he was when they arrived in Bethlehem a few weeks later. Finding a place to stay was a hassle, and as it turned out, all the precautions he'd taken with Mary's delicate condition didn't have much of an effect. She didn't weather the trip well. As he was looking for a place to stay, his patience grew thin and his options were low. The inn was full. Despondent, Joseph took the next best option that was presented to him and they were finally able to rest from their journey. He looked over at Mary. She gave no indication that she was upset at having to be in a stable. It seemed like she was just happy to get off the donkey she'd been riding on for so long. Yet there was something else in her face that took him a few minutes to decipher, but he soon realized what it was.

It was time.

WHEN JESUS WAS BORN, they wrapped him in swaddling clothes and laid him in a manger. Shortly afterwards, there was a commotion at the entrance. When Joseph went to investigate, he found shepherds standing there, all of them talking at the same time, making it difficult at first for Joseph to know what they were saying. With a great deal of effort, he managed to get their account of events that took place that night. He stood aside and allowed them to go see the child, and as they did so, Joseph stood off to the side. *The story of the shepherds was incredible*, he thought. Joseph marveled at it all, and went on to think about the angel's visit to Mary, then the dream he had, and now the miraculous events taking place at the birth of Jesus. *Surely there would be no doubt in anyone's minds as to the deity of Jesus*, he thought in wonder.

Many other events took place, including the arrival of wise men that brought gifts to Jesus. Joseph and Mary felt overwhelmed at the amount of attention that the birth of Jesus brought, but because of their knowledge of who He was, they were not surprised.

Joseph was to have another dream not long afterwards.

An angel appeared in his dream and said, "Arise, take the young Child and His mother, flee to Egypt, and stay there until I bring you word. Herod will seek the young Child to destroy Him."

When he woke up, Joseph acted swiftly, and stayed in Egypt with Mary and Jesus, just as the angel had instructed him. When they heard about the massacre of all the innocent children, he spent hours consoling Mary.

"I'm a mother, and I cannot begin to imagine what they're all going through. My heart aches for all those parents who lost their children."

"Hush now…," Joseph consoled, "…we're safe. All we do now is wait on the Lord for instruction."

True to his word, the angel again appeared to Joseph and told him to go to the land of Israel. "Those who sought the young Child's life are dead," the angel told him.

It was a glorious moment for them. The time to leave Egypt had come.

On their way to Israel, Joseph learned something that troubled him. Herod's son Archelaus had taken over from his father. Thinking that Herod's resentment would have rubbed off on his son, Joseph changed his plans. He decided to go to Nazareth instead.

For years things went well.

TWELVE YEARS CAME AND went before a significant episode became a vivid reminder to Mary and Joseph that Jesus was no ordinary boy. They had gone to Jerusalem just like they did every single year for the Passover feast.

On their return, a troubled Joseph told Paul, who had become his right hand man, what happened during the trip.

"We went to Jerusalem as usual," Joseph explained, "When we finished the days, Jesus stayed behind."

"He's only twelve years old. Why would He do something like that?" Paul asked.

Joseph pushed his hands over his face. He still remembered the fear that gripped him when he realized that Jesus wasn't anywhere to be seen. He sighed heavily.

"We didn't immediately realize that He wasn't with us. You know how we all travel together. For all we knew, He could have been with our parents, or some of His friends... anybody...," Joseph trailed off. He'd felt like kicking himself over and over because of what happened. It was up to him to protect his family, and he'd felt so helpless in those moments.

He went on to say, "Of course we went back to Jerusalem."

"But you found Him? Right?" Paul asked.

"We found Him. Three days later."

Paul folded his arms and gave a low whistle, then said, "Three days... That's a long time to spend looking for a child. How did Mary take it?"

"She was beside herself. Frankly, I wasn't doing too well myself. We had a lot of people looking, but that wasn't any consolation."

"I understand. The bottom line is that you found Him. Was He okay?" Paul asked.

"Yes." Joseph took a deep breath.

"And?"

"We found Him in the temple."

"The temple? I suppose that's not a bad place to find a child."

"Yeah, well, we were worried. He was sitting in the midst of the teachers, both listening to them and asking them questions."

"He must have asked good questions if they were staying around to be with Him," Paul observed.

"They told us that they were all astonished at His understanding and answers."

"Surely that's a good thing? You're a man who lives by the scriptures," Paul said cautiously. Having not felt the anxiety with them, he didn't see why it was a problem for Jesus to be with men who studied the scriptures.

Joseph didn't respond immediately, but when he did, he said, "Mary asked Him why He'd done this to us. She told Him how we searched. Jesus told her that He had to be about His Father's business. He asked why we were searching for Him."

"Joseph, you may not want to hear this, but we all know that Jesus is wise beyond His years. Those teachers would not have wasted their time if he didn't have something of substance to share."

"I know that. It just takes some getting used to. He's growing up."

Joseph was correct. Time sped by.

MARY RETURNED FROM a wedding in Cana of Galilee and told her friends about a miracle that took place there. "I told Him that they ran out of wine, and I instructed the servants to do whatever He told them."

"What happened?" her friend asked.

"Well, the obvious. They ended up having more wine. Jesus got them to fill the water-pots up with water. Then he had them take it to the master of the feast...," Mary was saying, but her friend interrupted to add the rest of what she thought would happen.

"I can guess. When he tasted it, the water was wine."

"That's correct. That's exactly what happened."

She listened as Mary gave a detailed account of the rest of the event. Everyone was amazed at the quality of the wine. It didn't surprise her friends, for they didn't expect anything less from Jesus.

As time progressed, Mary tried to keep track of what Jesus was doing. She constantly heard reports of even more miracles. People were being healed. The masses were following Him.

On the other hand, she also heard how those in power positions sought to destroy Him. Her concern grew.

There came a point when Mary felt that she could not take it anymore. She feared that Jesus would be stoned. There was a fine line between what the scriptures said and what the Pharisees tolerated, and in her understanding, Jesus may well have passed over that line.

Mary called her sons to her, and together they went in search of Jesus. They found Him surrounded by a multitude of people. People recognized them, and before long the word reached Jesus that His mother and brothers were there.

"Who is My mother, or My brothers?" Jesus asked and then looked around at those around Him, before He added, "Here are My mother and My brothers! For whoever does the will of God is My brother and My sister and mother."

The word went back to Mary, and when she heard the words, she felt shocked. Not knowing what else to do, she took her sons and went back home.

That night, Mary cried bitterly, feeling that she'd lost her son. She prayed, but even in her prayer, she didn't know if she was being effective. After the miraculous birth, she knew that Jesus would be destined for greatness. What she didn't understand then was the risks that would be involved.

She continued to hear of the things Jesus did, being astounded by the reports that came back to them.

Then it happened. She received the news that Jesus was captured at Gethsemane the night before. Mary acted as fast as she could. She had to be there. Judging from what she heard, they were trying to pass judgment as soon as they could. By the time she made it there, she found herself in a crowd that was screaming for Jesus to be crucified.

Her heart raced, and she pushed forward, trying to get a glimpse of him. She heard a deafening cheer going up in the crowd.

She pulled at the person next to her and asked urgently, "What's going on?! Why are they cheering?!"

A man turned to her and laughing shouted, "They're freeing Barabbas!"

Her heart skipped a beat. She wanted to know what that meant. Tears welled up and blinded her.

She kept pushing.

For a while she didn't see Him, and she frantically tried to get information from those around her.

Surely they knew that He was the Messiah, she thought, and continued to push through the crowds.

Then she caught a glimpse of Him through her tears.

She pushed some more.

His badly beaten body was covered in blood that oozed out of different wounds on His body. She wasn't close enough, so she kept pushing. Mary saw the cross that was being carried, and she desperately pressed onwards.

All of a sudden she felt hands grabbing for her.

"Mary! We found you! Mary!"

She turned around and saw her sister, and Mary Magdalene.

"Oh! Help Him!" Mary exclaimed then cried inconsolably.

They took her with them to Golgotha and held her close as the nails were driven in the hands and feet of Jesus.

A large crowd had gathered to watch the crucifixion, but Mary was only aware of the pain and suffering of Jesus. At some point, a few of the disciples of Jesus came to stand with her. They didn't know how to bring comfort, when they themselves were feeling shattered by what they were witnessing.

They raised the cross up. Vaguely, Mary noticed a cross to the right and a cross to the left of Jesus. Everything else was blotted out.

Jesus looked at her and she heard Him say, "Woman, behold your son!" At His words, she looked around and saw the disciple whom Jesus loved. She heard Jesus tell him, "Behold, your mother!"

As soon as the words were spoken, Mary felt the disciples arms go around her as she cried. He led her away.

The disciple took Mary home, and tried to console her as best he could, but he felt helpless. It was an honor to be chosen by Jesus to look after Mary, and it was an honor that he didn't take lightly. She looked like a woman who didn't have any more cry in her. They spent the next few days at home. As was the custom, mourners came to spend time with her, but every time it was Mary who sent them away, preferring to mourn the death of Jesus alone. They listlessly went about their chores.

IT HAD BEEN THREE DAYS.

Someone was banging on the door and shouted, "He's risen!"

The disciple looked at Mary, but she was still staring at the table.

The banging sounded, and more shouting, "He's alive! The tomb is empty! They say that He's risen!"

He jumped up and so did Mary. Then he swung the door open wide and saw that several people had gathered outside their door.

"He's risen!"

Her lips quivered. Mary looked at the disciple next to her, and then she told him, "I remember hearing that He said that He would pull the temple down and rebuild it in three days. This is the third day. He did it!"

The disciple smiled and replied, "Yes, Jesus did it!"

Don't miss out!

Visit the website below and you can sign up to receive emails whenever C.Orville McLeish publishes a new book. There's no charge and no obligation.

https://books2read.com/r/B-A-GABRB-KFLKE

BOOKS 2 READ

Connecting independent readers to independent writers.

Did you love *Mary & Joseph: A Christian Novel*? Then you should read *Chloe: A Christian Novel*[1] by C.Orville McLeish!

[2]

Chloe's life seems perfect. She has found true love, is an active member of her church, and her extraordinary talent for writing is on the brink of making a monumental impact. The movie she wrote is set to be released, promising to spread the gospel to an audience far and wide, potentially changing countless lives and bringing her dreams to fruition.

However, beneath the surface of this idyllic existence lies a hidden truth that threatens to unravel everything. Chloe's mother, Mary, harbors a secret so devastating that it could strip

---

1. https://books2read.com/u/3RlexR

2. https://books2read.com/u/3RlexR

away all that Chloe holds dear. As Chloe stands on the cusp of fulfilling her destiny, the revelation of Mary's secret looms ominously, ready to shatter Chloe's world.

In this gripping tale of faith, love, and redemption, Chloe must navigate the treacherous waters of truth and deceit. Will her faith and resilience be enough to overcome the impending storm, or will Mary's secret destroy the life Chloe has so carefully built?

Read more at https://clevelandomcleish.com/.

Also by C.Orville McLeish

Christian Youth Faith-Walkers Series
Detour: A Christian Novel
The Preacha And The Prostitute: A Christian Novel
Agents of Christ: The Prodigal Daughter: A Christian Novel
Chains: A Christian Novel
The Waiting Room: A Christian Novel
Chloe: A Christian Novel
Mary & Joseph: A Christian Novel

Made in God's Image Series
The Path to Spiritual Enlightenment
You Are Born To Win

The Unshakable Series
FAITH: A Theological Memoir

Standalone
Girl Unknown
Who I Am In Christ Daily Devotionals
How to Receive Your Healing
Sons of God: A Study on the Biblical Narrative of the Sons of
God
Made in God's Image: We are Partakers of God's Divine Nature
A Glorious Church: In Pursuit of the Biblical Model of
Christianity
The Seer: A Supernatural Christian Novel
The Soul of Man: Traversing the Mystery of Man as a Living
Soul
Exit the Matrix: Embracing Our True Nature as Born-Again
Christians

Watch for more at https://clevelandomcleish.com/.

About the Author

C. Orville McLeish is a successful entrepreneur, and an acclaimed multi-award-winning author, playwright, and screenwriter. He is a professional ghostwriter, copy editor and self-publishing service provider. With a deep commitment to intellectual and mystical theology, he intertwines his passion for health, fitness, longevity, and Christian spirituality. A proud graduate of Writer's Digest University and the School of Kingdom Mysteries, Cleveland is currently pursuing a master's in theological studies at Gordon-Conwell Theological Seminary.

Read more at https://clevelandomcleish.com/.

About the Publisher

HCP Book Publishing has been providing writing and self-publishing coaching, consultation, and services to new and seasoned authors since 2018.

Read more at https://hcpbookpublishing.com/.